Book No. 4

Gladys the C
and
The Slippery Slope

Written by
Elsie Bell

Illustrated by
Ray Schofield

Gladys the Dragon Series
edited by
Roger Wickham

Pond View Books

About these stories

Gladys is a sleepy, friendly dragon who doesn't fly any more. She will tell you she has 'quite given it up'. But in her dreams she **does** fly and, in some of her adventures, she flies off to a castle of long ago where a young girl called Lady Gwendolyn lives.

The dragon's best friend is George, an eight year old boy who lives near the farm where Gladys has made her home in a small cave on a rocky hillside.

In the first book, we found out how the dragon got her name - do you remember? In Book 2, Gladys saved Daddy's cricket match, but in this story we find Gladys on a slippery slope.

Gladys has many more adventures.

I hope you enjoy them all.

Elsie Bell.

This is where Gladys and George live.

The Slippery Slope

George loved the winter, especially when it snowed or when there was plenty of ice for sliding.

Living next door to George was a toddler called Ginger. Everybody called him Ginger because he had a huge mop of ginger hair. He had a special hat and scarf that he really loved.

There was a black and white penguin on the hat, and two more penguins on the scarf. Ginger wore the hat and scarf every time he went out, and sometimes he waddled along pretending to be a penguin himself. He looked very funny.

He loved them so much that he was especially happy if there was a penguin in his bedtime story. After the penguin stories, Ginger always insisted on going to bed in his special hat and scarf.

Ginger loved his special hat and scarf.

George made a slide one day when the ice was hard and thick on the hill. He took a good run at it and then stood at the top of the slide, with his arms spread out to help him balance, and whizzed right down the hill.

George's friends came to play on the slide and, as the weather got colder, the slide got even slidier. When it snowed, some of the children stood at the bottom of the hill and threw snowballs at the one who was sliding down.

They all had rosy cheeks and were enjoying themselves so much that they wanted to be outside all day long, playing in the snow.

However, one morning Ginger was in tears and had a different hat on and no scarf at all. He had raced about so much playing snowballs the day before, that he had fallen asleep in his push chair. Nobody had noticed when his special hat and scarf fell off. They were left out all night and had frozen into the ice at the top of the slide.

It was no use trying to pick them up, the ice was so hard that the hat and scarf were stuck fast.

All the children slid down the hill.

George managed to stop Ginger crying by explaining that the birds were upset too. The water in the birds' dish had frozen so hard that the poor birds couldn't have a drink.

Some of the grown ups were also quite dismayed when they saw how slippery the hill was. Every time they tried to walk up or down, they fell over. Ouch!

George decided it was time to find the dragon. He hadn't seen Gladys for days, and there were plenty of jobs for her.

Cold weather is no problem for dragons. All they have to do is get their r-r-rumbly breathing going and quite soon there is warm air all around.

Gladys was very cosy. She had just warmed up her cave and was enjoying a quiet snooze when George woke her up.

Gladys was very cosy in her cave.

"Gladys, we need you," said George. The dragon opened one eye, then closed it again and went back to sleep. She **really** didn't want to leave her cosy home.

"Gladys, wake up, PLEASE, we have lots of important jobs for you."

Gladys liked the sound of the word **'important'** and decided to investigate. "I'll come with you and see what I can do," she said.

The dragon sounded quite important herself as she set off with her best friend George across the snow.

When they got to the top of the hill, Gladys was amazed to find herself sliding crazily down the ice all the way to the bottom. The children laughed as the dragon landed in a heap at the foot of the hill.

"Goodness me, whatever has been happening?" said Gladys. She had never been on a slide before and wasn't quite sure if she liked it.

Gladys slid all the way down the hill.

George explained first about Ginger, whose favourite hat and scarf were stuck fast in the ice. Ginger was getting quite cross again because he could see them as clearly as anything but he couldn't pick them up!

But Gladys had noticed the poor birds who couldn't have a drink because the water in their dish had frozen and turned to ice.

The dragon knew just what to do. She started her warm r-r-rumbly breathing, but unfortunately she went on too long. The ice melted, then the r-r-rumblies got so warm that all the water dried up and disappeared. Gladys blinked in amazement when she saw the dish was dry and empty.

But George was clever. He simply scooped up a huge handful of snow and dropped it in the warm dish. The snow melted at once and turned to water, giving the birds a good drink.

The birds had a lovely drink from their dish.

George's mother wanted to walk down the hill, but the day before she had slid halfway down and nearly fallen.

She had been carrying a basket of shopping, and there were eggs in it. She had looked like a skater as she managed to keep her balance and hold on to the basket at the same time. She had saved the eggs, but the washing up liquid had shot out of the basket, burst open, and spread all over the ice.

Gladys looked at the hill. She could see that this was a bigger job than melting the ice in the birds' dish, and was wondering whether to start at the top or the bottom.

She decided to start at the top, and soon got the r-r-rumblies going in fine style. But at first the ice only melted slightly, and Gladys kept on wobbling and sliding down the hill herself.

Then, an amazing thing happened.

14

George's mum looked like a skater.

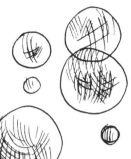

The ice began to melt and turn to water, but, as it warmed up, beautiful bubbles began to float about everywhere. The children were delighted.

Jessie and Johnny raced about chasing the lovely bubbles and trying to catch them. But it's not easy to catch a bubble, as they soon found out.

Everyone was laughing and making so much noise that the grown ups came out to see what was going on. Soon, everyone was sliding around and playing with the bubbles.

Where did all the bubbles come from, do you think?

George's mother realised it was the washing up liquid she had dropped the day before that was now turning to bubbles. But the children thought it was magic.

Gladys was very happy to see everybody having so much fun.

The children chased the bubbles.

Ginger had forgotten about his frozen hat and scarf in all the excitement. He raced and slid all over the place, blowing the bubbles about.

At last, all the bubbles floated away over the rooftops, the ice melted, and the hill was clear again.

All the people who had been wanting to walk down the hill came out now and gave Gladys's nose a grateful stroke. This was so soothing that Gladys fell asleep where she lay.

Now the excitement was over, Ginger remembered his special penguin hat and scarf trapped under the ice. George told Ginger to be patient, and that Gladys would help him when she had had a little snooze.

But Ginger was never patient. He always wanted things to be done that very minute.

So, what do you think he did?

18

Bubbles floated away over the rooftops.

Ginger was a cheeky little monkey!

He started to throw snowballs at the dragon, but Gladys simply did a little r-r-rumbly breath which made the snow melt on her nose.

Ginger thought it was very funny, and carried on with this game until Gladys woke up at last.

George took Gladys to the place where the hat and scarf were frozen in the ice, and it only took two warm r-r-rumbly breaths to melt the ice enough for Ginger to rescue his favourite penguin hat and scarf.

And after all that excitement and hard work,
I expect you can guess what Gladys did then,
can't you?

Yes. She fell asleep again at once.

Ginger threw snowballs at the dragon.

 George looked on in surprise as Ginger lovingly wrapped the scarf around the sleepy dragon's neck, and put the hat on Gladys's head.

"You can have them, Gladys, for being such a kind and helpful dragon," he said.

Gladys woke up. She knew how much Ginger loved his special penguin hat and scarf, and suggested that they should share them.

So they did. They took it in turns to wear them each day until all the ice and snow had melted away.

THE END

Ginger put his scarf around her neck.

TITLES AVAILABLE NOW

1. Gladys the Dragon and The Lost Lamb	1 871044 65 0
2. Gladys the Dragon in Gladys Saves the Day	1 871044 66 9
3. Gladys the Dragon and The Flying Lesson	1 871044 67 7
4. Gladys the Dragon and The Slippery Slope	1 871044 68 5
5. Gladys the Dragon meets Lady Gwendolyn	1 871044 69 3
6. Gladys the Dragon and The Mountain Bike	1 871044 70 7

More titles available Summer 1998

Order copies from your usual bookseller